Just Four

Femdom Hypnosis and Mind Control Micro-Fiction

S.B.

She needs more pets.

Thank you to all patrons of Spell… B-O-U-N-D.

Table of Contents

Introduction

Hypnotic women are always looking for new toys to play with and you want to be one so badly. The road to blissful submission won't be easy, but that shouldn't stop you from pursuing your wildest dreams. Prime your mind for what you need.

You can do that by reading yet another collection of mesmerizing micro-fiction filled with delicious temptations. Bit by bit, you'll become what you're meant to be. Give in now and have fun.

Almost Ready

Hans opened his eyes, vivid thoughts flaring. Men weren't servants! They didn't have to wear collars and submit to their girlfriends or wives. It was all a lie!

"Reverting again, huh?" Carmen noted, syringe in hand.

The needle pushed deep; memories came undone. Only three awakenings in the last twelve months. He was almost ready.

Old Triggers

Victor opened the last bag in the attic and exclaimed:

"Fuck!"

"What's wrong?" Brandon asked.

"It's one of Marie's music boxes. She used to trigger me with these."

"So? It's been three years, man! Aren't you over her already?"

"I don't know."

"Let's find out..."

Brandon's ass has never been the same since that day.

Oblivion Drop

Dean stood against the bedroom wall, mindlessly repeating:

"I must obey Goddess Carmen. I must obey Goddess Carmen..."

It was all he could say. Whenever the words brushed his lips, he fell deeper into trance, compelled to keep going until she was pleased.

Goddess Carmen checked her watch and smiled. Ten more hours should suffice.

No Glitch

Frank stared angrily at his laptop screen. The download was taking forever for fuck's sake!

Without a second thought, he rebooted the system, the blue background fading into liquid spirals, each one more attractive than the other. He sank and froze.

His mind will never run again without his girlfriend's permission and that's no glitch.

Being Thankful

"What are you thankful for?" Jack asked.

"The fact that my Mistress is away." Graham replied.

"That's horrible! Why?"

"She said she would hypnotize me into becoming a turkey if we were together on Thanksgiving."

"Really? What else did she say?"

"That I don't have a friend called Ja... shit!"

Graham gobbled all night long.

Sapphires Shine Brightest

It is not the stars that shine brightest but sapphires, sparkling radiance inside one's mind.

Look at them, your eyes drooping, thoughts melting in perfect harmony. Your soul is one with their reflections.

Life is but a flicker of hypnotic blue and the only thing it wants is your surrender.

It's time to give in.

Trading Secrets

The two friends sat on the sofa, drinking coffee.

"They seem to be getting along just fine." Allison noted.

"Did you have any doubts?" Helena asked.

"You know how pets can be..."

"I train mine well. Want to share brainwashing secrets?"

"Yes, please!"

They continued the friendly banter while their men chased their dicks around.

Sunday Movie

Cameron sighed. The movie was good but exceedingly long. Thirty minutes less and nothing of value would be lost... except the main female character's spiraling eyes, the confusion induction, the strikingly hot forced masturbation scene... oh, fuck!

"Huh? What do you mean it's over already?" he kneeled in front of the TV, begging for more.

Hallucination

"I can't believe the year is almost over..." Graham said.

"It was quite the crazy ride, huh?" Bill noted.

"Indeed, especially that time I hallucinated..."

"What do you mean?"

"Once, I believed Alpha males were real and I was one of them, but then Goddess showed me the light."

"Not the pendant?"

"That came next."

He's Not Brainwashed

I'm not brainwashed, he muttered to himself as he started thinking and obsessively dreaming about her every single day.

I'm not brainwashed, he said as his ego shrunk alongside any scattered thoughts of defiance or resistance to her wishes.

I'm not brainwashed, he concluded as he happily presented itself to her to be devoured whole.

A Christmas Gift

"Would you look at that!" Caroline said.

"What is it?" Jim asked.

"Daphne's husband bought her a new car. He's such a good man!"

"Ah... I can't afford one right now."

"You can't even afford a tricycle!"

"Untrue! I can buy a motorcycle at least."

"Perfect. Just what I wanted for Christmas. Thanks!"

Jim sighed.

Slave to Black

Daniel stared helplessly at the glowing computer screen, absorbing new truths without complaining.

Women were genetically superior, especially black women. Nia was the most beautiful black woman in the world. Nia deserved to have white boys at her feet at all times.

He drooled as his sense of self liquefied, another slave for her pleasure.

Keeping a Promise

Ralph knocked helplessly on the door.

"Wendy, let me in! It's cold!"

"Not until you keep your promise!"

"I did! You hypnotized me yesterday!"

"The deal was all December and today, you said 'no'! Now, it's my turn!"

"But..."

Silence fell as the blizzard grew stronger. Half an hour later, he agreed with two months.

Say My Name

The sorceress shook Bill and said:

"Hold the staff and say my name so my power flows to you."

"I don't know your name!"

"Slave."

"Seriously?"

"Yes, hurry!"

"Okay."

Bill touched the staff, looked at her and said:

"Slave?"

Lightning cracked the Earth as he fell to his knees. He was such a gullible man-child!

Backseat

Trevor's backseat gaming was getting obnoxious.

"Go left! No, your other left! No, back! What are you doing? God, why are you so dumb?"

Leanne laid down the controller, grabbed her pocket watch and said:

"Keep going and you're the one being played instead."

Trevor's eyes lit up as he added: "Nearly there, please continue..."

Person of the Year

Jonah stared quizzically at the busty redhead woman on the cover of Time.

"Why is she Person of the Year? I don't know her."

"Opening paragraph of the article." His brother replied.

"Mistress Veronica, Hypnodomme, wins this distinction for enslaving all men and then making then forget about it." Jonah read.

His eyes went blank.

Hypnotic Conversation

"We're not having this conversation again, Claire!"

"What conversation, Mark?"

"The one where you say you're hypnotizing me this weekend, I refuse, and then you do it, anyway."

"Jumped the gun there. I wasn't going to say that."

"What were you going to say then?"

"My sister's in town."

"And...?"

"She's hypnotizing you this weekend."

Mesmeric Lust

Thomas moaned heavily. Mrs. Danes was riding his cock, dropping him in and out of trance with each passing breath.

He blinked to face the ceiling of his empty bedroom. Another dream or perhaps a memory from college years resurfacing. He didn't know, but who cared?

Closing his eyes again, he surrendered to mesmeric lust.

Weird Taste

Will laid down the cutlery and muttered:

"This pizza tastes weird."

"Don't like anchovies?" Gretchen asked.

"Love them but is that all you put in it?"

"What were you expecting?"

"Knowing your kinks, some mind-control drug or something."

"I would never ruin a pizza like that."

"Good."

Too bad she never said anything about dessert.

Just Four

"I love your new shoes!" Clarice exclaimed.

"Thank you." Ashley responded. "A hypnoslave bought them for me."

"And the purse?"

"Another hypnoslave."

"The jacket too?"

"Yep."

"Wow! How many hypnoslaves do you have anyway?"

"Just four... for now."

"What did the other one give you then?"

"She's about to buy me dinner."

Clarice silently complied.

Shock Treatment

The sudden jolt made Peter's balls spring to attention.

"What was that for?"

"You were having nasty thoughts about women again." Barbara replied.

"No, I wasn't!"

"Are you calling me a liar?" She zapped him again.

"No."

"What do you say then?"

"Thank you for the discipline, Mistress."

"Good."

He was slowly learning his place.

Head Start

"Happy New Year!" Denise exclaimed.

"Remind me again why we're celebrating two weeks early." Her sister whispered.

"Mike said he would be my hypnoslave on January 1st."

"But he's already entranced!"

"I know. Just getting a head start... Look at him, already kneeling. Isn't he cute?"

Vanessa nodded and sat down to enjoy the show.

Favorite Movie

The Mason twins sat around the fireplace discussing Christmas movies with Dennis and new girlfriend, Carissa.

"Nothing beats Die Hard." Bob said.

"Bah." Victor retorted. "Love Home Alone 2."

"Mine is Holiday Pets." Carissa smirked.

"Huh? What's it all about?" The twins asked in unison.

Carissa reached for a pendant, and they got their answer.

Sweet Medicine

Jonah swallowed two pills with a glass of water. His head still hurt from the morning concussion, but his thoughts were getting clearer.

Dr. Winters was such a lovely woman, always looking out for him. He had to pamper and obey her.

He took two more pills and continued to fall deeper under her control.

The Present

Barry shook the early Christmas present. As he did, the wrapping paper came undone.

"One peek won't hurt, right?" He thought.

He opened it and sighed. Nothing except a note from Ava and a whiff of her perfume.

"Empty, just like you. I knew you couldn't resist." It read.

Barry smiled as his thoughts disappeared.

Interesting Dreams

Carrie waved a hand before her brother's blank eyes.

"Is he really under?"

"Absolutely." Willa replied.

"Now what?"

"Do whatever you want."

"And he won't resist?"

"No. He's too suggestible and yearns to be used. He has... interesting dreams with you, sometimes."

"Me too."

"Get busy then." The hypnotist smirked and closed the bedroom door.

Prelude to Eternal Bliss

"How do you do it, Hank?" Mark asked.

"Do what?"

"Stay so positive all the time."

"Easy. When darkness surrounds me, I stare into Judith's eyes. When her eyes stare back, I sink and let go."

"That sounds like hypnosis."

"It does."

"Why am I feeling dreamy right now?"

"Good question."

Judith entered the room.

Not What He Had in Mind

Horace stared at Nicholas' erect cock and exclaimed:

"This is embarrassing!"

"Most definitely."

"I swear this is not what I had in mind for your birthday. I thought she was a stripper!"

"In a way, she is. She did strip our ability to resist..."

"Right..."

"Less talking and more sucking, boys." Goddess Valeria, Hypnodomme extraordinaire, sneered.

Quite the Haul

Maîtresse Veronique inspected the batch of manservants and asked:

"Are these the last ones?"

"Negative." Brandi replied. "We've received intel of a group hiding in Taos."

"How many?"

"Hundred and fifty, perhaps more."

"Quite the haul. Do we have enough dresses?"

"We never run out of those, Maîtresse."

"Let's bag and brainwash some sissies then."

Almost Over

Walter exited the bedroom, fuming. The year was almost over and so was his patience. Katie was going to pay for enslaving him for so long. He would...

"... stare into my eyes and go deep once more?" She sneered.

"Y-yes." He stammered, resistance fading away. The year was almost over, but his servitude was eternal.

Change of Mind

The conditioning had not gone as expected. She'd wanted a more caring and thoughtful lover but, by screwing with the machine's basic configurations whilst the process was taking place, all she'd gotten was a broken mind, reduced to blind sexual obedience. The end result was unfortunate…

Her mind changed dramatically right after the tenth orgasm.

The Only Truth

He was silently dazzled when the computer screen turned black, the sequence of pictures and words gone from view, but extremely vivid within his mind. Next to him, towering in latex and shiny boots, was a striking woman he recognized from her title alone.

"I'm your Owner!" she proclaimed, her words becoming his only truth.

Laundry Day

It was Laundry Day again and everyone in the mansion knew its meaning. All the dutiful slaves hurried to the Conditioning Room in the top floor and, one by one, entered the machine designed to reinforce the feelings of submission towards their Mistress.

The minds of thralls need to always be clean, don't you agree?

The Core

"You won't take us!" Jeremy shouted to the apparently empty, white room. He couldn't see them but felt them there. Holding Helena in his arms, he wasn't sure if he believed his own words.

"Yes, we will." responded the voice of one thousand consciousnesses. "You'll be broken. No one resists The Core!"

And they didn't.

Seven Slaves

"We're so glad you're here." Doc said with a smile as the other dwarfs nodded their approval. "Now you can cook for us and tend the house while we work in the mine!"

"Nope, not going to happen…" Snow White answered as she gave them a glance of her mesmerizing breasts.

The seven slaves knelt.

Scientific Breakthrough

Science is a dangerous invention of mankind, and some of its creations should have never come to life. I discovered a way to turn people into docile servants just by having them read the things I write, but I can't seem to reverse the process.

So, you know what that means….

Kneel and obey, slave!

The Other

I don't want to fall asleep. Because when I do, that's when The Other takes control, a body without a mind, a numb replica deprived of will, and I'm forced to watch its surrender to the whims of others, screaming from the inside but never being heard.

I won't fall asleep… I… *yawn*… must… *yawn*…

Oriental Seduction

"And now, you're completely under my control!" whispered the Chinese beauty as the crystal pendulum came to a halt. "Henceforth, you'll obey my every command, do you understand?"

"Yes", answered a dull voice.

"State your purpose in life, then!"

"To serve you forever, Mistress!"

"Exactly! Now, go get the palanquin. I want to go shopping!"

The Final Game

Jack was about ready to reach ten million points but, at the deciding moment, his hands shook the table a little too hard and the dreaded word TILT flashed red as the flippers stopped working and the last ball fell out of sight.

"I've just won a new slave…" cooed the demoness next to him.

Alien Force

This will be my final entry in this journal.

For many months, I fought the dreary visions that assaulted my brain, but I feel that my mental training is finally beginning to fail.

Soon, I shall become the embodiment of submission to an alien force that's undying and invincible.

And, one day, so will you.

The Final Lesson

Wrapped up in plastic, in a dark room, unable to move….

Then, she comes in: a latex-clad femme fatale with flowing, black hair….

The sight of her makes me tingly, eager to kneel.

I want it to happen, but first I need to complete my training.

"Ready for your final lesson?" she asks, smiling mischievously.

The Greatest Inventor

They say Nicolas Flamel discovered the secrets of the Philosopher's Stone to turn lead into gold.

Just the other day, my friend Mark found a way to change copper into platinum, believe it or not.

I transform willful men and women into my devoted, mindless subjects with my computer programs.

Who's the greatest inventor, huh?

Reshaped

On all-fours inside a vacuum cube, I feel the latex sheets sapping all strength to resist. My arousal is so intense that I can no longer think straight. All I know is I'm being reshaped into the plaything I was always meant to be.

I hear a door swing open. Bliss! My Owner has returned!

No Longer Alone

I used to be sad and alone all the time, lost in meaningless self-imposed thoughts of misery.

Then, I met her. In her words I found solace like no other, and in her spellbinding eyes, I discovered gateways to the endless promises of love.

I'm no longer alone. I wish you all the same luck.

Secret Box

This wooden box?! I bought it at an auction for three hundred thousand dollars! It would have been a waste of money if it didn't come with a secret... All I have to do is open it up in front of anyone I choose and... voilá! Instant sex slave, eager to please....

Best deal... ever!

The Bet

The rules of the board game Rachel had chosen were of Byzantine complexity, and Derek was at a loss as to what to do. It was now clear he was going to lose the bet.

"Oh, why did I agree to become her slave for the weekend if I lost?" he thought.

Rachel grinned, sexily.

Disappearing Act

"I hate that you chew gum all the time!"

"Tough luck! What are you going to do about it, Nadine?"

"A bit of magic, obviously! Alakazam! See? All gum is gone, including your secret stash!"

"What the hell?! How did you do that?!!"

"I told you: Magic! Now, wait until I make your mind disappear.... "

Wonderful Opportunities

Jessica Lynch was prone to accidents: a broken window here, a car crash there, and lots of complications everywhere, really!

Of course, sometimes, accidents turn out to be wonderful opportunities, like when she mixed some chemicals and spilled a strange concoction all over herself.

Try googling 'Mistress Jessica Bitch' to see exactly what I mean.

Big Words

"So... did you like my erotic story?" Bonnie asked, nervously.

"Hmmm... frankly, I stopped reading right after 'The Brobdingnagian paramour entered the sweltering halls...'" Sheila answered with a smirk.

"Huh? But that's only the beginning of the first sentence!"

"I know. It turns out my patience is quite Lilliputian when it comes to big words...."

For Starters…

"Bill, I'm tired of doing all the work around here, so it's time to delegate."

"I don't like the sound of this, but... What do you want me to do, Rachel?"

"For starters, you can bathe the cats."

"The cats?! But I'll be scratched to no end!"

"Aren't you the one that loves wet pussies?"

Rehabilitation

"How are you feeling, today?"

"Strange... diminished... like a piece of me is missing..."

"And in a way, it is. Those desires of dominance were a major part of your life for a long time. The Process will fix that!"

"Are you sure?"

"Positive. Soon, you'll be the slave you were always meant to be."

The Right Qualifications

"Congratulations, Number Twelve. You passed the test with flying colors and are now officially qualified to be a horny slave for all eternity, just like you always wanted. Feel free to express the orgasmic satisfaction you're feeling right now in any way you see fit, preferably naked and on your hands and knees... good girl!"

Preparations

"What do you mean 'my opinions are irrelevant'? I helped design this thing!"

"We know, Mr. Phelps. However, you don't get to tell us how we use it. Just be thankful we let you keep your free will."

He gulped, looking at the apocalyptic machine.

She was right.

Soon, many others wouldn't be so lucky.

The Truth

For eons, I sought the truth, the elusive word from which all dreams are born. Countless times, I despaired by the abyss and then... you saved me.

Now, looking at you on your throne, hearing your voice echo within, I know that word instinctively, and will repeat it gladly until I die.

Love, Love, Love...

The End

"Ten seconds for impact, nine, eight..."

"It seems this is the end, everyone. It was a pleasure to serve with you all," said the Captain trying his best to keep his composure.

"One, ze...."

In a heartbeat, the bomb detonation wiped out the individuality of all men and women in a five hundred mile radius.

Conclusion

Well? Aren't you feeling positively entranced right now? Of course, you are, and this wonderful sensation will continue for as long as you wish it. In the meantime, be sure to visit my personal website - https://www.sbspellbound.net - for more fantasies waiting to be unleashed. Consider supporting my creative efforts if you want even more. Thank you in advance.

www.ingramcontent.com/pod-product-compliance
Lightning Source LLC
Chambersburg PA
CBHW071448150726
48000CB00006B/2479